W9-CBK-640

My "p" Sound Box®

(Blends are included in this book.)

Library of Congress Cataloging-in-Publication Data
Moncure, Jane Belk.
My "p" sound box / by Jane Belk Moncure; illustrated by Colin King.
p. cm.
Summary: A little girl fills her sound box with many words that begin with the letter "p."
ISBN 1-56766-782-1
[1. Alphabet.] I. King, Colin, ill. II. Title.
PZ7.M739 Myp   2000
[E]—dc21   99-054327

My "p" Sound Box

Jane Belk Moncure

illustrated by Colin King

The Child's World

Little  had a box.

"I will find things that begin
with my 'p' sound," she said.

"I will put them into my sound box."

Little 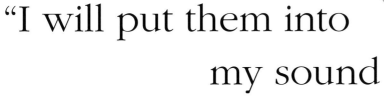 found a poodle

and her puppy.

Did she put the poodle and the puppy into the box?

She did.

Then Little  found a  pig . . .

and  piglets

in a pigpen.

Did she put the pig and piglets into the box with the poodle and the puppy? She did.

Little walked down a path to the park.

In the park, she saw a tree with peaches. She put some peaches into her box.

Under the peach tree

Little

saw a picnic table and a picnic basket.

"Lets have a picnic," said Little  P.

She opened the picnic basket and found

peanuts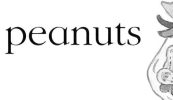

pickles

popcorn

and pie.

Little  and the animals ate

until the pig said,

"I am about to pop!"

Little put the animals
back into the box.

She also put back the leftover peanuts, pickles, popcorn, and pie.

Now the box was so heavy,

it was about to pop!

Then Little  saw a pony pulling a cart.

"Please pull us!" she said.

The pony pulled them down the path.

They saw a . . .

porcupine.

Little gave the porcupine some popcorn.

She put him into the box . . .
carefully . . . because he was prickly.

The pony pulled them on down the path.

Soon they saw a peacock.

Little  gave the peacock some peanuts.

Then she put him into the box.

Suddenly, the pony stopped.

A panther

was in the path!

The pony pranced! The pig, piglets,
poodle, puppy, peacock, and porcupine
fell out of the box.

The panther pounced

on the box.

He ate up all the peanuts, pickles, peaches, popcorn, and pie!

Then he smiled politely.

Just then,
a policeman
came down
the path.

"You have found our pet panther," he said.
"We will take him back to the zoo."

"Let's take all of my pets to the petting zoo,"

said Little

They had a parade . . .

picnic basket

poodle

pony

peacock   porcupine   piglets

all the way to the petting zoo.

peaches

policeman

puppy

pig

panther

path

Can you read these words with Little  ?

pretzel

pencil

panda

paste

parrot

plane

pelican

puppet

parachute

plate

penguin

pocket

piano

29

ABOUT THE AUTHOR AND ILLUSTRATOR

Jane Belk Moncure began her writing career when she was in kindergarten. She has never stopped writing. Many of her children's stories and poems have been published, to the delight of young readers, including her son Jim, whose childhood experiences found their way into many of her books.

Mrs. Moncure's writing is based upon an active career in early childhood education. A recipient of an M.A. degree from Columbia University, Mrs. Moncure has taught and directed nursery, kindergarten, and primary grade programs in California, New York, Virginia, and North Carolina. As a former member of the faculties of Virginia Commonwealth University and the University of Richmond, she taught prospective teachers in early childhood education.

Mrs. Moncure has travelled extensively abroad, studying early childhood programs in the United Kingdom, The Netherlands, and Switzerland. She was the first president of the Virginia Association for Early Childhood Education and received its award for outstanding service to young children.

A resident of North Carolina, Mrs. Moncure is currently a full-time writer and educational consultant. She is married to Dr. James A. Moncure, former vice president of Elon College.

Colin King studied at the Royal College of Art, London. He started his freelance career as an illustrator, working for magazines and advertising agencies.

He began drawing pictures for children's books in 1976 and has illustrated over sixty titles to date.

Included in a wide variety of subjects are a best-selling children's encyclopedia and books about spies and detectives.

His books have been translated into several languages, including Japanese and Hebrew. He has four grown-up children and lives in Suffolk, England, with his wife, three dogs, and a cat.